Contents

Written by Brian Roberts
Illustrated by Pat Reynolds

M000104771

Sally's Bad News Day

It all began one sunny day in April. Sally's parents shared the news at the dinner table that the family would be moving in eight weeks. Sally's mother had been offered a new job which was just too good to turn down. Sally wanted to be happy for her mother, but her first thoughts turned to the friends she would leave behind.

Friends are important to a ten-year-old, and Sally was sad at the thought of leaving them. Her stomach began to churn, and suddenly her dinner didn't taste so good. A big tear rolled down her cheek. She left the table and went to her room, where she cried and cried.

Sally's mother understood Sally's feelings. When she was about Sally's age, the same thing had happened to her. So she went to Sally's room to comfort her.

Before long, Sally's dad came in, too. He tried to make her feel better by telling her that she would get her own room in the new house, instead of sharing with her younger sister. But, at that moment, nothing was going to make her feel better, not even her dad's hugs.

Sally was what you might call a tomboy. She loved playing basketball and soccer. If she wasn't playing one of these sports, she was climbing trees, riding her skateboard, or collecting insects.

It had taken a long time for her to be accepted by the boys who lived near her. For some reason, boys around eight to ten never think a girl can play sports as well as a boy can. But Sally was determined to prove them wrong, and she did. She wondered whether she would have to prove herself all over again in the new town.

Moving Day

Eight weeks seemed like a long time, but they passed quickly. Soon it was moving day, and Sally's friends came to say goodbye. Although Sally was still sad about leaving, she had come to accept the move and was kind of excited. Sometimes a combination of feelings can be confusing, and Sally wrestled with the combined feelings of sadness, fear, and excitement.

Sally waved goodbye to her friends as she and her family drove away. They had promised to e-mail each other when Sally got to her new town. They had even made plans to visit during the summer. But Sally knew that things would never be the same. She would have to make new friends.

The next day, Sally and her family pulled up in front of their new home. It was a much bigger house. Sally jumped out of the car and ran to the door. She yelled back to her dad, "Hurry up! I want to see my new room."

As her dad unlocked the front door, Sally bolted through it. She ran from room to room. "Which one's mine?" she asked excitedly.

"The big corner room upstairs. The one that looks out over the pond," replied her mother.

"Cool," said Sally. "I must have the coolest room of any ten-year-old in the world." And, at that moment, any feeling of sadness was replaced with excitement.

Making Friends

It wasn't long before curious kids in Sally's new street came to the house to check out the new family. First came a group of four boys about Sally's age. They didn't seem to show much interest in Sally. Instead, they asked if she had any brothers. When she said no, that she only had a younger sister, they walked away.

"Here we go," said Sally. "Boys must be the same wherever you go."

"What do you mean by that?" asked her mother.

"Boys think that the only people in the world worth knowing are other boys," Sally replied, scowling. "I guess I'll have to prove them wrong just like I did with the boys back in Nelsonville."

Sally went on moving into her new room. She put all the sports trophies she had won on the shelves. She hung posters of rock climbers and skateboarders on her walls.

11

When she was finished, she grabbed her skateboard and headed out to explore the new street. Whizzing by the field where some boys were playing soccer, her long hair flying behind her, she caught their attention.

"Wow, did you see that?" said one of the boys.

Sally skateboarded to the field the next afternoon. This time, she asked if she could play. But the leader of the group, a boy named Freddie, said, "Sorry, no girls allowed."

Sally had gone through this before, so she was not going to get discouraged. That evening, she told her dad she needed his help.

"The boys here are just like the ones in Nelsonville," she told him. "I have a plan. I need to show them I can play soccer as well as they can. They play every day at the field at about two o'clock. So, if you can come and kick some balls with me they'll see how well I can play."

"Sounds like a good plan to me," her dad agreed.

The next day, just before two o'clock, Sally and her dad went to the field. When the boys arrived, Sally was kicking the ball to her dad. The boys pretended they didn't see her, but she knew they were watching. After an hour, Sally and her dad quietly went home.

The Next Day

The next day, Sally returned to the field once again.

"Look," she said, "I know that you think a girl can't play as well as a boy, but I'm here to prove that I can. I just need a chance."

The other boys looked at Freddie. One of them said, "Come on. We all saw her passing the ball yesterday. She's good. Let's give her a chance."

"Yeah," said Billy. "Let's give her a chance. She could really help our team. Anyway, it can't hurt – we've lost all but one of our games this year."

Freddie told the team to come and huddle with him. "We can't just let her play," he said. "We have to make her do something to prove that she's worthy."

"Like what?" asked Billy.

"Like bringing us a sack full of snakes," said Freddie.

They all agreed that if she brought them a sack full of snakes, she would be allowed to play soccer with them. The group of boys strutted back to where Sally stood all alone.

"Here's the deal," Freddie said to Sally. "You can join the team, but only on one condition."

"So, what's the condition?" asked Sally.

"The condition is this," Freddie replied with a grin. "You catch, and bring to us, a sack full of snakes. Then you can play soccer with us. Do you think you're brave enough to do that?"

Sally looked Freddie straight in the eye. "No problem," she replied. "How much time do I have?"

"We'll give you a week. If you don't have the snakes by then, you can forget about joining the team," said Freddie.

Sally's Snake Hunt

Sally had hunted frogs, toads, bugs, lizards, and even snakes, since she was six. She kept them for a day or two, then always let them go.

Sally liked snakes best, and she had read many books about them. She knew where to look for snakes – the large pond near their house was a good place to start. She also knew which ones were dangerous.

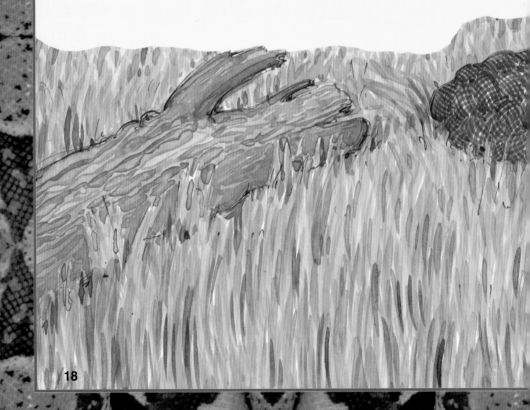

After about three days, Sally had caught 12 snakes. Most of them were garter snakes, which weren't very long. Sally wanted to find some bigger snakes, so for the next two days she went hunting in the fields at the edge of town. After two days she had caught a black racer, and two corn snakes.

When she thought she had enough snakes, Sally put them in a sack and headed for the shed where the boys hung out. When she knocked on the door, Billy answered. He smiled at her when he saw the sack slung over her shoulder.

"I've got your snakes," she said.

Billy stuck his head into the shed and told the others that Sally was there with the snakes. Freddie came out and the others followed close behind.

"So what have you got in the sack?" asked Freddie with a smirk.

"What do you think?" replied Sally. "A sack full of slimy spaghetti?"

"Let's see what you've got in there!" Freddie demanded.

Sally opened up the sack. Freddie could see more than a dozen snakes squirming inside.

"Well, it looks like you got a few snakes, but not enough," said Freddie. "If you want to play soccer with us, you need to catch more."

"That's not fair," shouted Sally. "We had a deal, and I brought you the sack of snakes you asked for."

"She's right," said Billy. "We had a deal with her and she did what we asked."

"Shut up, Billy," said Freddie's friend, Frankie. "Freddie makes the decisions around here, and he say she needs to bring more snakes."

Sally grabbed the sack, threw it over her shoulder, and stomped off in anger.

Sally Gets Even

Sally wasn't going to let Freddie have his way. She had completed her part of the deal, and one way or another she was going to play soccer with them. And there was one thing for sure – she wasn't going to catch any more snakes for Freddie. She didn't trust him.

Later that day, after the boys had left, Sally went back to the shed. She looked around very carefully, and after a while she came up with a plan.

The next day, Sally put the snakes back into the big sack, threw it over her shoulder, and headed for the team's shed. She hid in the bushes and watched the boys leave one by one. Soon they had all gone except for Freddie, and that other boy, Frankie. Sally didn't like Frankie, either. He was a big bully, too, and he helped Freddie with his dirty tricks.

Sally sneaked up to the shed and quietly rigged the door so that it wouldn't open. Then she climbed a tree next to the shed and crawled onto the roof.

"What's that up on the roof?" yelled Freddie. "What's going on?" He tried to get out the door but it seemed to be jammed shut.

Just then, Sally opened a hatch on the roof and emptied all the snakes from the sack into the shed.

Freddie and Frankie began screaming and yelling.

"Let us out of here!" screamed Freddie. "I'm afraid of snakes. Let us out! Let us out!"

"Only on one condition," said Sally.

"What is it?" he asked. "Anything. You can have anything you want. Just let us out of here."

"You know what I want," said Sally. "I just want to be treated fairly. I want to play soccer with you."

"OK, OK," said Freddie. "I promise you can play. Just get us out of here."

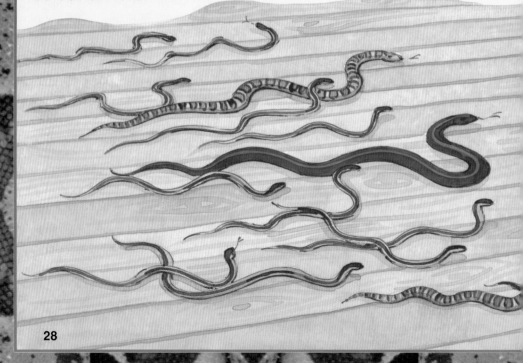

Sally climbed down off the roof and let the boys out. They ran off as fast as lightning. Next, Sally went into the shed, gathered up the snakes, and put them back into the sack. Then she went back to where she had gathered the snakes from and set them free.

The next day, Sally showed up for her first soccer game. She scored two goals and the team won their first game in six weeks. Sally was the hero. Even Freddie and Frankie thought she was pretty cool!